The Time Traveller Book of PHARAOHS AND PYRAMIDS

Tony Allan
assisted by Vivienne Henry

Illustrated by Toni Goffe
Designed by John Jamieson

Contents

2	Going Back in Time	18	Setting Sail for the Court
3	The People You Will Meet	20	At the Pharaoh's Court
4	A Trip to Ancient Egypt	22	Battle!
6	Along the Nile	24	A Warrior is Buried
8	At Home with Nakht	26	The World of the Spirits
10	Giving a Feast	28	The Story of the Pharaohs
12	Visit to a Temple	30	How We Know About Egypt
14	Going to School	32	Index
16	A Trip to the Pyramids		Further Reading

Going Back in Time

There are plenty of ways of going back in time. You do it every time you go to a museum or a castle and try to imagine how people used to live many years ago. Or you can do it by looking at pictures and books. That is what this book is about.

It takes you on a trip back to the very beginning of history. The people of ancient Egypt were among the first to leave behind pictures and writings showing how they lived. It is by looking at them that we can know what ancient Egypt was like.

In this book you are going to make a journey back in time. It is as if you had been given a magic Time Helmet to take you to Egypt as it was nearly 3,400 years ago. On the next page are the people you will meet when you are wearing it.

The Time Travelling Helmet

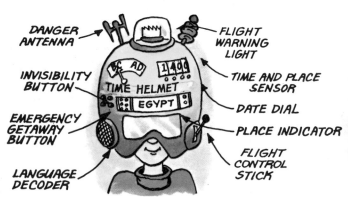

This is the Magic Time Travelling Helmet. You can go back to any time you want, simply by setting the time and place controls. This time you are going to Egypt as it was in the year 1400 B.C.

This is Your Destination

Egypt is in the north-east corner of Africa, south of the Mediterranean Sea. You have to go back 33 centuries. Below are a few stop-off points to show you how things change when you jump back in time

This is north-west Europe in 1940, about the time your parents were born.

Things have not changed very much, but notice the aeroplane and the radio.

You have gone back another 40 years. Things are quite a bit different.

There are oil-lamps, lots of decorations, and the women wear long clothes.

Now a big jump over 400 years. The only lighting is by candles, and all the heat comes from a big open fire. Most of the furniture is plain, and the window is made of tiny panes of glass.

This time you have moved in time and place, to Rome in 100 A.D. You have already gone back nearly 1900 years, but you still have almost as far to go again. Ancient Egypt is the next stop.

The People You Will Meet

The Egyptians all live within a few miles of the River Nile. It is warm and sunny most of the time, so they do not need to wear many clothes. Children hardly ever wear clothes at all.

The rich people have pleasant lives. They live on big estates, where servants and slaves do much of the work. But most of the people are poor peasants who must work hard to live.

Tiy has been married to Nakht for twenty years. She is called Mistress of the House, and has to look after it and take care of the children. All the furniture and household goods belong to her.

Nakht is a wealthy landowner who lives in a big house a few miles up the Nile from the city of Memphis. He often has to go to the city, because, like his father before him, he is in charge of the lands of a temple there.

Shery the eldest daughter, is a lively girl of 13. Because she is a girl, she does not go to school. But she is taught what she needs to know at home as well as singing and dancing.

The Pharaoh is the ruler of all Egypt. His subjects believe that he is a god in the body of a man, and think that he can do no wrong. He is so revered that people have to kneel down before they speak to him.

Mosi, their eldest son, is 16. His father wanted him to train as a scribe, but Mosi wants to be a soldier. Nakht has finally agreed to this, and has promised to introduce him to a general he knows.

The youngest daughter is called Meu, which means 'kitten'. She is 8 years old. She has little to do but play in the garden all day.

The vizier is the Pharaoh's chief helper. It is his job to see that the ruler's orders are carried out.

Scribes earn their living by knowing how to read and write. Some work for the army, others in temples or on private estates. They organize the work other people do.

Hori, the youngest son, is 10. He is learning to be a scribe, and goes with his father to Memphis to attend the temple school. He expects to take over his father's job after Nakht has retired.

Ahmose, Nakht's nephew, is staying with his uncle's family. His own father has gone on a long trading voyage to Byblos, a port across the Mediterranean Sea in Lebanon.

Priests work in the temples, looking after the gods. They have to keep themselves pure and clean. They bath four times a day, shave their bodies, and dress in the finest linen.

Most Egyptians are peasants. They have to work hard to grow enough food to live on, and have to pay taxes to the Pharaoh's officials. If they fail to pay, they are beaten. They normally have enough to eat, but when the harvest fails the Pharaoh sees that they are given grain from his Treasury.

Most of Nakht's servants are free to leave him if they want. But some are slaves. They are the children of foreigners captured in wars.

Soldiers lead hard, dangerous lives. But a few successful ones may become rich and famous generals.

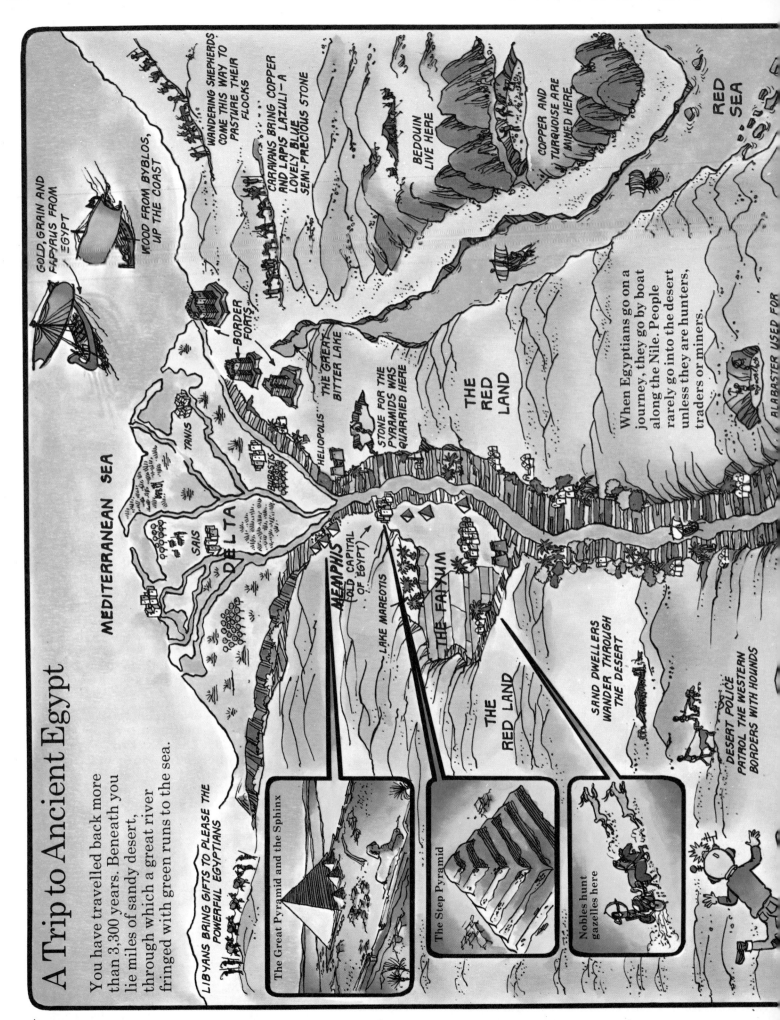

A Trip to Ancient Egypt

You have travelled back more than 3,300 years. Beneath you lie miles of sandy desert, through which a great river fringed with green runs to the sea.

GOLD, GRAIN AND PAPYRUS FROM EGYPT

WOOD FROM BYBLOS, UP THE COAST

WANDERING SHEPHERDS COME THIS WAY TO PASTURE THEIR FLOCKS

CARAVANS BRING COPPER AND LAPIS LAZULI – A LOVELY BLUE SEMI-PRECIOUS STONE

BEDOUIN LIVE HERE

COPPER AND TURQUOISE ARE MINED HERE

RED SEA

MEDITERRANEAN SEA

BORDER FORTS

TANIS

HELIOPOLIS

THE GREAT BITTER LAKE

STONE FOR THE PYRAMIDS WAS QUARRIED HERE

THE RED LAND

When Egyptians go on a journey, they go by boat along the Nile. People rarely go into the desert unless they are hunters, traders or miners.

SAIS

DELTA

BUBASTIS

MEMPHIS (OLD CAPITAL OF EGYPT)

LAKE MAREOTIS

THE FAIYUM

THE RED LAND

SAND DWELLERS WANDER THROUGH THE DESERT

LIBYANS BRING GIFTS TO PLEASE THE POWERFUL EGYPTIANS

DESERT POLICE PATROL THE WESTERN BORDERS WITH HOUNDS

ALABASTER USED FOR

The Great Pyramid and the Sphinx

The Step Pyramid

Nobles hunt gazelles here

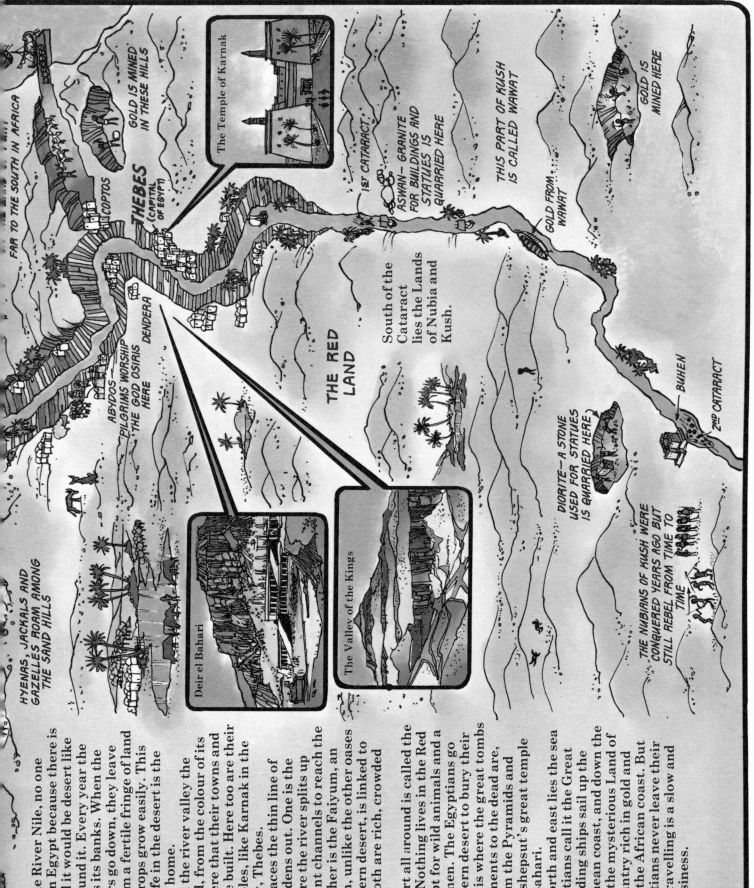

FAR TO THE SOUTH IN AFRICA

HYENAS, JACKALS AND GAZELLES ROAM AMONG THE SAND HILLS

GOLD IS MINED IN THESE HILLS

COPTOS

THEBES (CAPITAL OF EGYPT)

The Temple of Karnak

ABYDOS— PILGRIMS WORSHIP THE GOD OSIRIS HERE

DENDERA

Deir el Bahari

The Valley of the Kings

THE RED LAND

South of the Cataract lies the Lands of Nubia and Kush.

1st CATARACT

ASWAN— GRANITE FOR BUILDINGS AND STATUES IS QUARRIED HERE

THIS PART OF KUSH IS CALLED WAWAT

GOLD IS MINED HERE

GOLD FROM WAWAT

DIORITE—A STONE USED FOR STATUES IS QUARRIED HERE

BUHEN

2ND CATARACT

THE NUBIANS OF KUSH WERE CONQUERED YEARS AGO BUT STILL REBEL FROM TIME TO TIME

Without the River Nile, no one could live in Egypt because there is no rain and it would be desert like the land round it. Every year the river floods its banks. When the flood waters go down, they leave behind them a fertile fringe of land on which crops grow easily. This thread of life in the desert is the Egyptians' home.

They call the river valley the Black Land, from the colour of its soil. It is here that their towns and villages are built. Here too are their great temples, like Karnak in the capital city, Thebes.

In two places the thin line of green broadens out. One is the Delta, where the river splits up into different channels to reach the sea. The other is the Faiyum, an oasis which, unlike the other oases in the western desert, is linked to the Nile. Both are rich, crowded places.

The desert all around is called the Red Land. Nothing lives in the Red Land except for wild animals and a few tribesmen. The Egyptians go to the western desert to bury their dead. That is where the great tombs and monuments to the dead are, among them the Pyramids and Queen Hatshepsut's great temple at Deir el Bahari.

To the north and east lies the sea —the Egyptians call it the Great Green. Trading ships sail up the Mediterranean coast, and down the Red Sea to the mysterious Land of Punt, a country rich in gold and incense on the African coast. But most Egyptians never leave their country. Travelling is a slow and difficult business.

5

Along the Nile

It is late in the year. The flooded waters of the Nile are going down. After three months with little to do, the peasant farmers are busy again, sowing seed for next year's harvest.

Another urgent job is to repair the canal banks. There is very little rain in Egypt, so water cannot be wasted. A system of catch-basins has been built, in which the flood overflow can be stored and used during the rest of the year to water the fields. It must not be allowed to drain away.

The river itself is busy with boat traffic. It is the land's main highway, and all heavy things, like statues and stone for building, are carried down it in sailing ships and barges.

People use it for private journeys too. The boat of Nakht, coming from Memphis, has just turned off the river. He is going home to the villa where he and his family live.

STATUE OF PTAH FOR A TEMPLE

FISHERMEN

Fishermen in boats made of papyrus reeds trawl the river for their dinner. There are many fish in the Nile. They make a tasty addition to a normal diet of bread and beer.

THE PHARAOH ROPE STRETCH REMEASURE FIELDS

NAKHT

WOODEN PICK

Canals are useful for travelling, and also because they carry water to fields far from the Nile. They must be kept in good repair.

Nakht is rich enough to have his own wooden boat. Wood is expensive in Egypt because not many trees grow there.

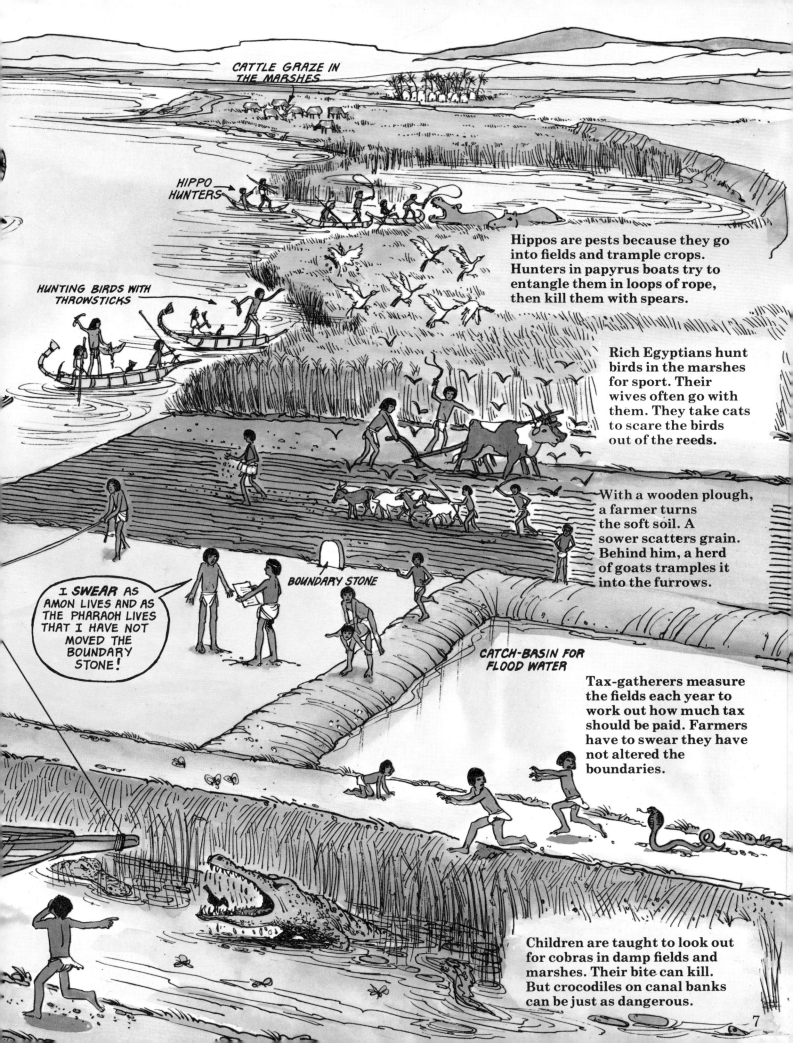

CATTLE GRAZE IN THE MARSHES

HIPPO HUNTERS

HUNTING BIRDS WITH THROWSTICKS

Hippos are pests because they go into fields and trample crops. Hunters in papyrus boats try to entangle them in loops of rope, then kill them with spears.

Rich Egyptians hunt birds in the marshes for sport. Their wives often go with them. They take cats to scare the birds out of the reeds.

With a wooden plough, a farmer turns the soft soil. A sower scatters grain. Behind him, a herd of goats tramples it into the furrows.

I SWEAR AS AMON LIVES AND AS THE PHARAOH LIVES THAT I HAVE NOT MOVED THE BOUNDARY STONE!

BOUNDARY STONE

CATCH-BASIN FOR FLOOD WATER

Tax-gatherers measure the fields each year to work out how much tax should be paid. Farmers have to swear they have not altered the boundaries.

Children are taught to look out for cobras in damp fields and marshes. Their bite can kill. But crocodiles on canal banks can be just as dangerous.

7

At Home with Nakht

Nakht has arrived home. He lives with his wife, Tiy, and their family on a large estate. He owns a house and garden, a stableyard, and outbuildings where the servants live and where food is cooked.

He also owns a lot of farming land nearby. Peasants look after this for him, and in return have to give him some of the food they grow. Nakht has a steward to help him look after the estate. His job is to see that the peasants give Nakht what is due to him.

Nakht's house is built of mud bricks, like all Egyptian homes. These are simply mud mixed with sand or straw, then left to dry rock-hard in the sun. The walls of the house are whitewashed. The floors are raised to make it hard for snakes to get in.

In the house, a ring of outer rooms surrounds a central hall. The hall's ceiling is raised, so high windows can let in light and air. It is cool and shady inside, but the family spend much of the day out of doors.

COLLECTING HONEY FROM BEEHIVES

The walled garden round Nakht's house is looked after and watered by his many gardeners and slaves.

NAKHT

TIY→

WORKMEN PICK FIGS WITH THE HELP OF PET BABOONS

Important guests are entertained in the pillared reception room.

STEWARD

SCRIBE

DUCKS' EGGS

Peasants from the estate bring cattle and geese to be counted by Nakht's steward. Those who bring fewer than they should are beaten.

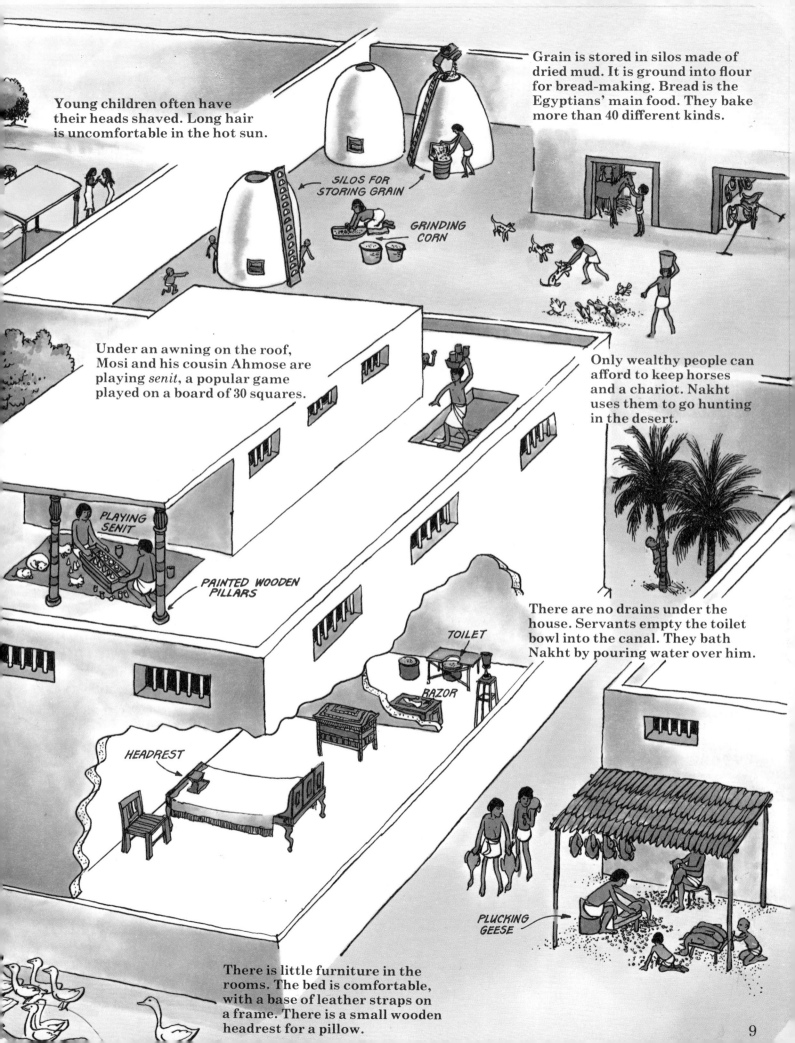

Young children often have their heads shaved. Long hair is uncomfortable in the hot sun.

Grain is stored in silos made of dried mud. It is ground into flour for bread-making. Bread is the Egyptians' main food. They bake more than 40 different kinds.

SILOS FOR STORING GRAIN

GRINDING CORN

Under an awning on the roof, Mosi and his cousin Ahmose are playing *senit*, a popular game played on a board of 30 squares.

Only wealthy people can afford to keep horses and a chariot. Nakht uses them to go hunting in the desert.

PLAYING SENIT

PAINTED WOODEN PILLARS

There are no drains under the house. Servants empty the toilet bowl into the canal. They bath Nakht by pouring water over him.

TOILET

RAZOR

HEADREST

There is little furniture in the rooms. The bed is comfortable, with a base of leather straps on a frame. There is a small wooden headrest for a pillow.

PLUCKING GEESE

9

Giving a Feast

Nakht has decided to give a feast to celebrate his return home. The Egyptians love parties, and never need much of an excuse to have one.

The guests are gathered in the central hall of Nakht's villa. Married couples sit together, but the unmarried are separated —boys and girls sit apart.

Singers and dancers entertain the guests, and servants bring round food. A lot of wine is drunk. Some guests drink so much that they have to be helped home.

All the guests wear perfume cones on their heads. These melt as the party wears on, drenching their wearers in sweet-smelling oils.

Servants pass to and fro among the guests, offering food and pouring wine. They give them flower garlands to wear round their necks and lotus blossoms to hold or wear in their hair. After the meal they will bring bowls of water for the guests to wash their hands in, because they eat the food with their fingers.

PET GOOSE

Preparing food

1 All the food for the feast is made by Nakht's servants. They make bread by kneading and shaping the dough, then baking it in flat cakes over a fire.

FIGS BREAD HONEYCOMB

2 Ducks and geese are both favourite meat courses. The birds are roasted whole over an open fire. The cook fans the flames to keep it burning.

3 Plenty of fruit and vegetables are grown on the estate. Figs, dates and grapes are the favourites. Honey is used to sweeten drinks and food.

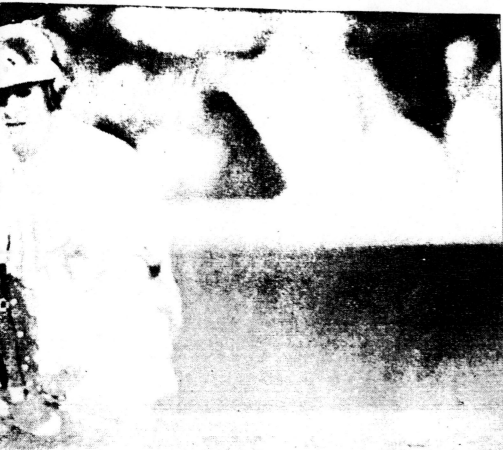

d's Terry Steinbach slides safely across the plate last night in the first inning.

Fun and a title

Juniors cruise in tennis tourney

What does Jared Lissauer enjoy about tennis? Well, he likes the exercise, the skill and competition.

Winning championships doesn't hurt either.

"I just like playing the game," Lissauer, 12, said yesterday. "I think it's fun to go out and hit the ball. I play four or five times a week."

Lissauer, a Central Middle School student, works hard on his game. Hard enough at least to win the town Junior Tennis Tournament's 14-and-under championship.

He accomplished that this weekend with a 6-0, 6-0 blanking of Aaron Stearns in the championship match. Lissauer needed only 45 minutes to turn the trick.

"My backhand was working; that and my second shot," Lissauer said. "My backhand is my strongest shot."

Lissauer dropped only four games in the entire tournament, all of those coming in a second-round match against Robby Mountain. Lissauer won that 6-1, 6-3 to earn a berth in the final. He blanked Scott Secord 6-0, 6-0 in a first-round meeting.

Lissauer regularly plays out of Shippan Racquet Club and takes lessons at Ivan Lendl's Grand Slam center in Banksville. He will enter the seventh grade this fall.

"It felt pretty good to win. It was especially nice to win the 14-and-under (tournament) as a 12-year-old," Lissauer said.

In other final matches, Peter McWhorter defeated Ben Stewart 6-3, 6-0 to claim the boys singles 12 and under championship; Terry O'Brien won by default from Andres Berghoist to win the boys 16 and under title; in the 12 and under girls singles, Suzanne Crowe defeated Abby Phillips 7-6, 6-4; in the 14 and under girls singles, Josephina Bercetche defeated Pamela Love 6-2, 6-0.

In the girls doubles, Laura and Jenny Hill lost to Pamela Love and Abby Phillips.

— Jim Smith

s just another ll where the opportunity to e Toronto. In just two of its

Got all that? Well, let's go back to the beginning when Oakland racked N.Y. starter Johnson to build that 8-1 lead.

"I made a lot of bad pitches," said Johnson, who threw 57 pitches (34 for strikes). "Lots of pitches. Lots of pitches in bad locations. You can't give up 10 hits in two-plus innings.

"It was one of those days. Everybody has them. This is my worst out-

Please turn to **YANKEES**, Page B8

loss

been thinking struggling," ood for me."
won for the ns, beating the nd time in a runs and eight truck out five y Rogers, who bases-loaded ghth, got four

s pounded for 6 1-3 innings. on its third in the first on le and Gonza-e 420-foot sign

RBI single in Palmer hit his e year in the

AP photo

Boston catcher Tony Pena, left, looks on as Texas Ranger Juan Gonzalez, right, is congratulated by teammate Julio Franco after Gonzalez hit a two-run home run in the top of the first inning.

Tony Pena hit a run-scoring double-play grounder in the fifth and seventh.

Gonzalez homered in the eighth

Shery gets ready for the feast

Before a mirror of bronze, Shery rims her eyes with a black powder called kohl.

She pounds red ochre into a powder to rub on her cheeks and palms.

Her servant hands her a wig. On top she puts a cone of perfume.

A blind harper waits to play when the dancing girls finish. His song is one of the oldest in Egypt. Make the most of time, he sings, for life is only a dream and all must die.

BLIND HARPER

WINE JAR

LOTUS BLOSSOM

PET MONKEY

Making wine

1 Most Egyptians usually drink beer, but rich people are also fond of wine. Most landowners have grapevines growing on trellises on their estates.

2 The grapes picked from the vines are taken to the press. While some workers trample them underfoot, others collect the juice that gushes out.

3 The grape juice is poured into pottery jars to ferment into wine. These are sealed with leaves and a cap of mud that bakes hard in the sun.

11

Visit to a Temple

The temple in which Nakht works is like a small city. It has its own workshops, school, library, granaries and storerooms. Outside its walls, which are built of stone, it owns many acres of farming land. Many people work for it, and depend on the food in its granaries and storerooms for their living.

The most important part of the temple is a small, dark room that only priests enter. It is the sanctuary where the god lives—for the Egyptians believe their temples are the homes of gods.

Ordinary people are not allowed to disturb the god. But they can go to the temple forecourt to make offerings to him. Or else they may go to the temple to work—like Hori. He has come to learn to read and write at the school.

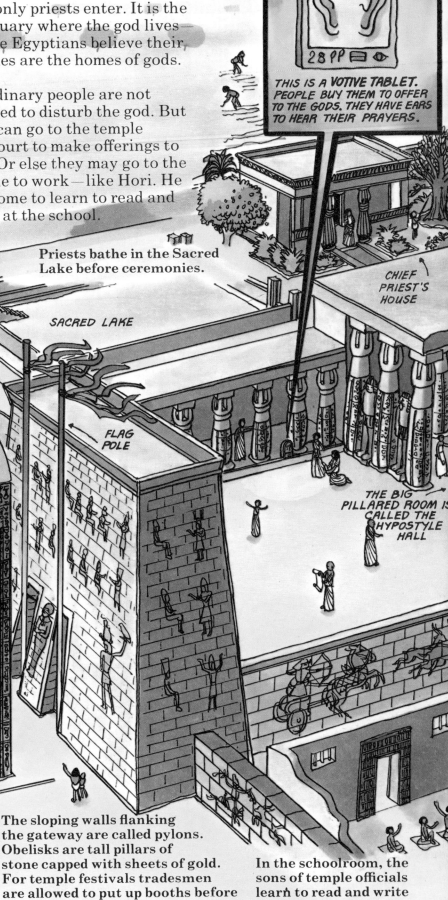

THIS IS A VOTIVE TABLET. PEOPLE BUY THEM TO OFFER TO THE GODS. THEY HAVE EARS TO HEAR THEIR PRAYERS.

Priests bathe in the Sacred Lake before ceremonies.

SACRED LAKE

CHIEF PRIEST'S HOUSE

FLAG POLE

THE BIG PILLARED ROOM IS CALLED THE HYPOSTYLE HALL

STATUE OF PHARAOH

PYLON

HORI

OBELISK

MAKING AN OFFERING

SETTING UP BOOTHS FOR A TEMPLE FESTIVAL

The sloping walls flanking the gateway are called pylons. Obelisks are tall pillars of stone capped with sheets of gold. For temple festivals tradesmen are allowed to put up booths before the pylons.

In the schoolroom, the sons of temple officials learn to read and write so that they can become scribes.

12

The Gods of Egypt

The Egyptians believe in many different gods. Once every city had a god of its own. Now there are some great gods, like Amon, whom all Egyptians worship. But people still feel loyal to the god who lives in the temple in their home town.

Here are three gods who are known in all the land.

AMON

Amon of Thebes is worshipped throughout the land as King of the Gods.

PTAH

Ptah, the god of Memphis, is the patron god of craftsmen.

BES

Bes, a comic dwarf god, brings good luck and happiness in the home.

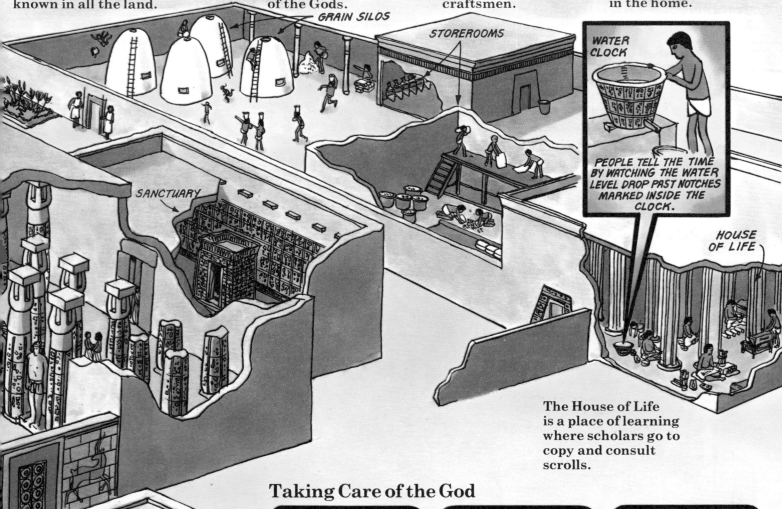

GRAIN SILOS

STOREROOMS

SANCTUARY

WATER CLOCK

PEOPLE TELL THE TIME BY WATCHING THE WATER LEVEL DROP PAST NOTCHES MARKED INSIDE THE CLOCK.

HOUSE OF LIFE

The House of Life is a place of learning where scholars go to copy and consult scrolls.

SCHOOL

WOMEN MUSICIANS PRACTISING FOR THE FESTIVAL

Taking Care of the God

1. The main temple ceremony is that of looking after the god. Each morning a priest, newly shaved and washed, enters the sanctuary.

2. He takes the statue of the god out of its shrine. He sprinkles water on it, changes its clothing, and offers it food and drink.

3. He puts it back in the shrine and leaves the doors open until evening. He goes out of the sanctuary, wiping away his footprints.

13

Going to School

Most Egyptian children never go to school. As soon as they are old enough to work, the boys go to work with their fathers. The girls learn how to run a home.

Hori goes to school because he is going to be a scribe, like his father. Scribes are proud of being able to read and write, and they make sure that their sons can carry on the tradition.

Hori does not find school much fun. There are no sports or games. He spends his days doing copies and dictations, and chanting texts aloud. He also learns to do sums. His teacher is strict. Egyptian schoolmasters have a saying that a boy's ears are on his bottom—he listens when he is beaten.

To cheer Hori up, his father tells him that his knowledge will make him rich and successful. The texts he studies will teach him the wisdom of the past, so he will become a good man. When he has learned to write, he can study foreign languages, history, geography and religion.

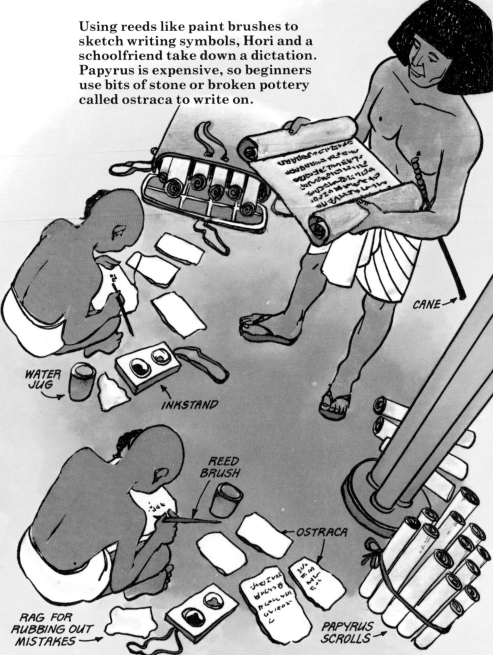

Using reeds like paint brushes to sketch writing symbols, Hori and a schoolfriend take down a dictation. Papyrus is expensive, so beginners use bits of stone or broken pottery called ostraca to write on.

WATER JUG

INKSTAND

REED BRUSH

OSTRACA

RAG FOR RUBBING OUT MISTAKES

CANE

PAPYRUS SCROLLS

1 Making Papyrus

The Egyptians make many things from papyrus reeds, including rope, sandals, baskets and boats. They also use papyrus to make paper. The tall reeds grow in marshy ground. Workmen cut them down and carry them away in bundles.

In the workshop the long reeds are chopped into short lengths (a). The green outer skin is peeled away (b). A workman then cuts the white pith inside lengthways (c) into wafer-thin slices, using a knife with a bronze blade.

POUNDING MALLET

CLOTH

POLISHING STONE

Two layers of pith are placed crossways on a pounding block. Th workman puts a cloth over them, and beats them into sheets with a mallet. To make a smooth writing surface, the sheets are finally polished with a stone.

Egyptian Writing

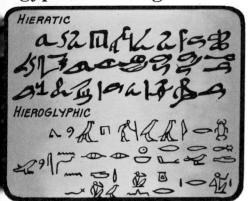

HIERATIC

HIEROGLYPHIC

WORD SIGNS

MEANING:
OLD MAN   JACKAL
SUN   HILL   COUNTRY

SOUND SIGNS

The Egyptians have two different kinds of writing—hieratic and hieroglyphic. Hieratic writing is a kind of shorthand, used for day-to-day business. Hieroglyphic writing, the older kind, is used for religious writings and for inscriptions on monuments. It is very difficult to learn.

As Hori will be a temple scribe, he has to learn hieroglyphic writing. Hieroglyphs are already about 2,000 years old. They were at first a picture language, in which there was a little drawing for each word. A small drawing of a boat meant 'boat'. It was quite easy to write simple messages.

As time passed, the writing became more complicated. Signs began to be used to stand for sounds, as the letters in our alphabet do. Words could be made up of several different signs. The picture above shows the main sound alphabet—but other signs are also used for groups of letters.

Learning to Read Hieroglyphs

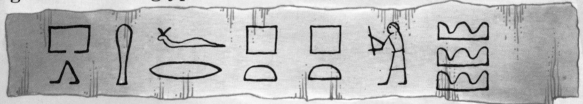

Hori spends a lot of time at school studying hieroglyphic inscriptions, to learn how to read the language. This one, like almost all of them, is a

mixture of sound signs and word signs. The Egyptians have no written vowels, so many words look alike. To help tell them apart, they often write

the sound of a word, then put a special sign, called a determinative, after it to make its meaning clearer. Here is what the signs mean.

  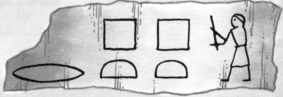 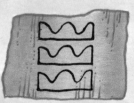

The word for 'house' sounds like the word for 'go forth', so the house symbol is used for both.
The walking legs show that here it means 'go forth'.

The club is a sound sign which means 'majesty'. The snake is the Egyptian letter 'f'. But it can also be used to mean 'his', as it does here.

The mouth symbol is the letter 'r' and, also, as here, the word for 'to'. The stool is the sound sign for 'p', the loaf of bread for 't'. Repeated, they spell the word for

'crush'. To make the meaning of the word clearer, a determinative sign for 'force'—a man striking with a stick—is tacked on at the end.

As Egypt is flat, the sign for 'hill' also means 'foreign land'. Here it is plural. The whole sentence reads: "Goes forth His Majesty to crush foreign lands."

KEY

WORD SIGNS AND DETERMINATIVES

(WALKING LEGS) GO
(MAN WITH STICK) FORCE
(HILLS) FOREIGN LAND

SOUND SIGNS

(HOUSE) STANDS FOR 'PR'   (MOUTH) STANDS FOR 'R'
(CLUB) STANDS FOR 'HM'   (STOOL) STANDS FOR 'P'
(HORNED VIPER) STANDS FOR 'F'   (LOAF OF BREAD) STANDS FOR 'T'

A Trip to the Pyramids

The pyramids were built more than a thousand years before Nakht was born. They are old and timeworn. Many of their outer stones have been stolen.

Yet they are still marvels. Most wonderful of all is the Great Pyramid of King Cheops, which stands on the edge of the desert across the Nile from Nakht's home.

During the flood season the waters of the Nile rise close to the Pyramid. Sight-seers like Nakht and his children can sail almost up to it, to pay their respects to the dead pharaoh and to visit the buildings.

1,200 Years Before—Building the Pyramids

One way of cutting blocks of stone for a pyramid was to cut notches in solid rock and then to hammer in wooden wedges. When water was poured on them they swelled, splitting off the blocks cleanly.

Most of the blocks for the Great Pyramid, weighing over two tons each, were quarried in the desert nearby. The white facing stones were carried on boats from the east bank across the Nile.

The ground where the pyramid was to be built had to be cleared of sand and stone. Workmen using ropes and sighting sticks dug channels which were filled with water to make sure the site was level.

The most difficult job of all was to raise the heavy stones into place. Most people think they were pulled up a huge earth ramp that was raised each time a new layer of stones was added.

When the pyramid was finished, the ramp was taken away. As the ramp went down layer by layer, workmen put white limestone facing stones on the jagged sides of the pyramid, to give them a smooth surface.

After many years' work, the pyramid was ready. When the Pharaoh died, his coffin was dragged up to the burial chamber inside it. Then the way into the pyramid was blocked and hidden.

Inside the Pyramid

The Great Pyramid is the biggest stone building ever built. It is made of more than two million huge blocks of cut stone. King Cheops had it built while he was still alive to keep his body safe after death. He stocked the burial chamber with treasures to use in the after-life—jewels and furniture, hunting equipment and food.

But despite his efforts, thieves have found their way in. There is nothing left inside the pyramid but the stone coffin in which he was buried.

SMALL PYRAMIDS FOR THE PHARAOH'S CHIEF QUEENS WERE BUILT BESIDE THE TOMB

A causeway links the mortuary temple to a second temple nearer the Nile. When the river is in flood, people can sail up to the lower temple. The dead pharaoh's body was carried to it by boat.

16

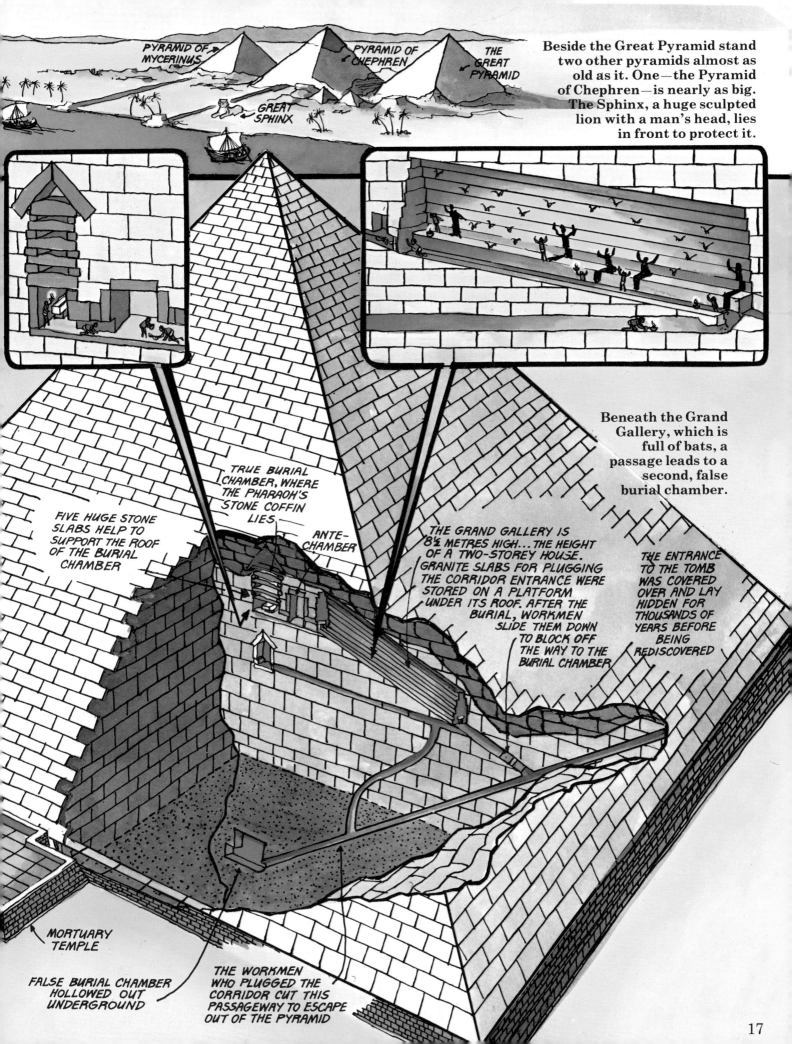

PYRAMID OF MYCERINUS

PYRAMID OF CHEPHREN

THE GREAT PYRAMID

GREAT SPHINX

Beside the Great Pyramid stand two other pyramids almost as old as it. One—the Pyramid of Chephren—is nearly as big. The Sphinx, a huge sculpted lion with a man's head, lies in front to protect it.

Beneath the Grand Gallery, which is full of bats, a passage leads to a second, false burial chamber.

FIVE HUGE STONE SLABS HELP TO SUPPORT THE ROOF OF THE BURIAL CHAMBER

TRUE BURIAL CHAMBER, WHERE THE PHARAOH'S STONE COFFIN LIES

ANTE-CHAMBER

THE GRAND GALLERY IS 8½ METRES HIGH...THE HEIGHT OF A TWO-STOREY HOUSE. GRANITE SLABS FOR PLUGGING THE CORRIDOR ENTRANCE WERE STORED ON A PLATFORM UNDER ITS ROOF. AFTER THE BURIAL, WORKMEN SLIDE THEM DOWN TO BLOCK OFF THE WAY TO THE BURIAL CHAMBER

THE ENTRANCE TO THE TOMB WAS COVERED OVER AND LAY HIDDEN FOR THOUSANDS OF YEARS BEFORE BEING REDISCOVERED

MORTUARY TEMPLE

FALSE BURIAL CHAMBER HOLLOWED OUT UNDERGROUND

THE WORKMEN WHO PLUGGED THE CORRIDOR CUT THIS PASSAGEWAY TO ESCAPE OUT OF THE PYRAMID

Setting Sail for the Court

Mosi is going to Thebes. His father Nakht has had to go to the capital on business at the Pharaoh's court. He has asked his son to join him there.

Mosi is leaving from a small trading post on the Nile. The boat he is to sail in is returning to Thebes after unloading a precious cargo of goods from the Land of Punt.

The Pharaoh has sent this as a gift for a temple nearby.

The village is busy. Sailors are unloading the ship, while scribes weigh and note down its cargo. In the marketplace above the harbour, stall keepers are doing good business. A group of wandering bedouin tribesmen have come in from the desert where they live to trade.

VENTS TO CATCH BREEZES

LEATHER WORKERS

MOSI

BARBER

SCALES

BEDOUIN

Because it is warm out of doors, people work and shop in the open air. There is no money, so shopping is done by barter. To decide what costly goods are worth, sellers work out their value in terms of fixed weight of gold, silver or copper called a *deben*. The buyer must offer something worth as many *deben* in exchange. The bedouins' donkeys are laden with dyed woollen cloths to exchange for food. The men have beards, and unlike the Egyptians they wear brightly-coloured clothes.

18

The cargo from Punt includes gold, elephant tusks (which will be turned into ivory ornaments), baboons, and incense trees for the priests to plant.

Egypt imports a lot of wood, because few big trees grow by the Nile. Most of it comes from Byblos, on the Mediterranean Sea's eastern coast.

TIMBER FROM BYBLOS

ELEPHANT TUSKS

SCRIBE

MIXING CLAY

BEDROLL

POTTERS AT WORK

KILN FOR BAKING POTS

Like the bricks of the houses, pots and jars are made from Nile mud. After an apprentice has trampled the mud into a paste, a skilled potter shapes it into vases that will be baked hard in the tall kilns.

Only wealthy people like Nakht have villas. Most people live in small, cramped houses with barely enough room for the family. In warm weather it is often more comfortable to sleep on the roof.

21

At the Court of the Pharaoh

Nakht has been ordered to attend a reception in the Pharaoh's palace in Thebes. Ambassadors from Syria are bringing tribute to the Pharaoh. Some of their gifts will go to Nakht's temple to honour the god Ptah.

Nakht is overcome with awe in the presence of the Pharaoh. Like all Egyptians, he worships his ruler. He believes he is the son of Amon. His word is law. It is an honour to be allowed to kiss the dust before his feet.

The young Pharaoh sits with his wife in the audience-hall. He behaves with the dignity expected of Egypt's ruler.

Yet secretly he is bored with the Syrians' flattery. He is more interested in Kush. He has heard rumours of a revolt, and is awaiting the arrival of his viceroy for the province. He knows that the news the viceroy brings could mean war.

The Syrians live in a mountainous land north-east of Egypt. They were conquered by the great Pharaoh Tuthmose III, and have been forced to send tribute to Egypt ever since.

Their envoys bring rich gifts, including a bear for the royal zoo. They also bring royal children to stay at court. Although the children will be treated well, they are hostages who will be killed if their parents rebel.

COPPER INGOT

A Day in the Life of the God-King

1 The Pharaoh's day begins early, because he has much to do. He is dressed by servants, and given the flail, the crook and the *nemes* head-dress—all symbols of royalty.

2 For Egypt to prosper, the Pharaoh must win the favour of his fellow gods. So he performs a ritual each morning in the temple, burning incense over an offering to Amon.

3 Much of the day is taken up with problems of government. Dispatches must be read and advisors consulted. The vizier helps to keep the Pharaoh informed.

The Crowns of Egypt

The Pharaoh wears different crowns for different occasions. This is the blue War Crown.

The White Crown is the crown of Upper Egypt. The Red Crown is the crown of the Delta region.

As ruler of all Egypt, the Pharaoh usually wears the Double Crown, which unites the Red and White.

The elaborate, top-heavy *hemhemet* Crown is worn only for temple ceremonies, if at all.

SCIMITAR

NAKHT

VICEROY OF KUSH

NUBIAN PRINCES

TRUMPETER ANNOUNCING VICEROY'S ARRIVAL

The Viceroy, whose official title is 'The King's Son of Kush', arrives with two loyal Nubian princes.

4 In the afternoon he goes to watch work on a temple he is building. The inside of the building is filled with rubble, over which the stone blocks can be hauled into place.

5 The Pharaoh enjoys going hunting, although this can be dangerous. The fiercest prey are lions. In ten years he has killed more than 100 of them.

6 Less tiring pleasures are waiting for him at home in the palace. Before going to bed, he plays a game of *senit*—a form of draughts—with his wife.

Battle!

The news from Kush is bad. Rebellious Nubian tribesmen in the far south have attacked a government outpost. The Pharaoh decides to send reinforcements to punish them.

An expedition is quickly organized. Most soldiers work in the fields in peacetime, so they have to be called up to fight. The crack soldiers are the charioteers, who have to provide their own chariots. But only a few will go to Kush. Carrying horses down the Nile on boats is difficult.

One of the soldiers called into service is Mosi. Although he is a new recruit, he has already been made a standard-bearer. He is eager for a chance to prove himself in battle.

1 The Pharaoh Calls the Men to Arms

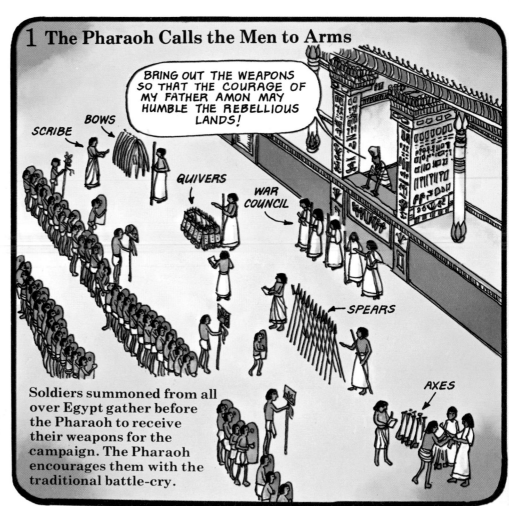

Soldiers summoned from all over Egypt gather before the Pharaoh to receive their weapons for the campaign. The Pharaoh encourages them with the traditional battle-cry.

2 The Expedition Camps by the Nile

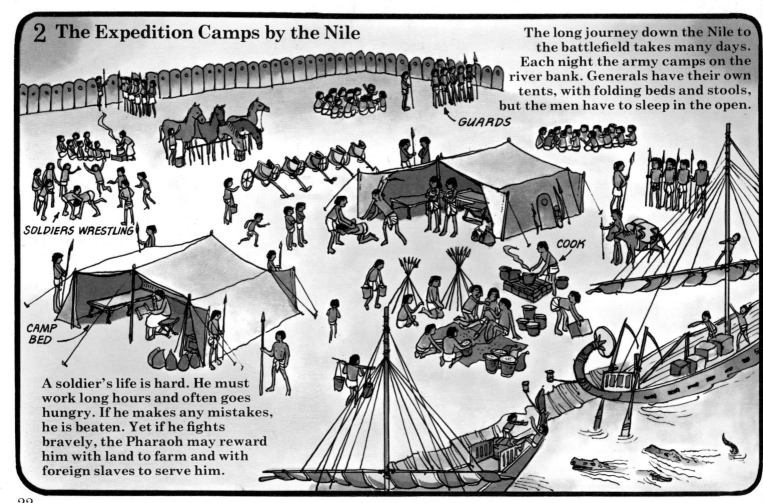

The long journey down the Nile to the battlefield takes many days. Each night the army camps on the river bank. Generals have their own tents, with folding beds and stools, but the men have to sleep in the open.

A soldier's life is hard. He must work long hours and often goes hungry. If he makes any mistakes, he is beaten. Yet if he fights bravely, the Pharaoh may reward him with land to farm and with foreign slaves to serve him.

3 Attack!

Archers begin the attack with a hail of arrows, then the foot-soldiers close in hand to hand. The Nubians, with their simple bows and clubs, are no match for the better-armed Egyptians. The fight is soon over. Then the chariots sweep by to chase the survivors from the field.

4 Spoils of Victory

Nubian captives are led away into slavery. Scribes count piles of hands cut from dead warriors—a grisly way of counting the enemy dead.

The Egyptian soldiers set fire to the Nubian encampment, and gather booty of food and animal skins.

A Warrior is Buried

The Egyptians won an easy victory in Kush, but some of their own soldiers were killed. One was a friend of Mosi's—a young Theban called Bata.

His grief-stricken parents have chosen to bring his mummified body back to Thebes for burial. They think he will be happier in the after-life if he is given a proper tomb.

The funeral procession makes its way to a tomb which his father had been preparing for himself. It is hollowed out of a cliff, west of the Nile.

Four priests—one of them wearing the mask of the jackal-headed god Anubis—perform the last rites over the mummy.

One priest 'opens' the mouth' of the mummy by touching its lips with a special tool. This is to give the dead man power to eat, speak and move in his next life.

MUMMY

WOMEN MOURNERS

FOOD FOR THE FUNERAL FEAST HELD AFTER THE BURIAL

CANOPIC CHEST

A big box called the canopic chest is put in the tomb with the mummy. Inside it are jars containing parts taken out of the dead man's body by the embalmers.

The women howl and throw dust over their heads. Some are relatives of the dead man, but others are professional mourners hired for the funeral. The men sit quietly and make little show of their sorrow.

24

1 Making a Mummy

To keep the body in good condition for the after-life, embalmers have special ways of preserving it. They take the brains and some inner parts out of it. Then they clean it and fill it with sweet-smelling spices.

2

Next they cover the body with a white powder rather like salt called natron. Bags of natron are packed around the head. The body is left for many days, until all the moisture left in it has dried out.

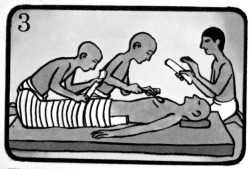

3

The body is then washed and wrapped in linen bandages. It is coated with oils and resins and adorned with jewels and charms. A mask goes over the face. Finally it is wrapped again, ready for burial.

The bier is shaped like a boat in honour of the boat in which the sun god Ra travels across the sky every day. The dead man may meet Ra in the after-life.

Oxen drag the bier up the rocky paths on the Nile's west bank that lead to the Theban burial-ground.

BIER

FURNITURE FOR THE TOMB

The Egyptians believe that life after death is much like life before it. So they make sure tombs are stocked with furniture, food, and everything a man might need to enjoy his death in comfort.

25

The World of the Spirits

Every Egyptian hopes for a life after death in which he will work, eat and drink just as he did on earth. His tomb is his home for the after-life, so wealthy people like Bata's parents take great care preparing theirs. Dead people must eat, so piles of food are painted on most tomb walls. People believe that the painted food will, by magic, stop them from being hungry.

First the dead man must pass a terrible test. Nakht tells his children what will happen to Bata in the world of the spirits.

Whenever Egyptians go on a journey, they go by boat. They believe that the sun too must travel in a boat to make its daily journey across the sky. They believe that

each night, after the sun has gone down over the western desert, the falcon-headed sun god Ra gets into another boat to sail over the world of the spirits.

1

Before he can live again, Bata must face a frightful ordeal. Like all dead people, he must go for trial before Osiris, the Lord of the Underworld. Only good people pass the trial; the rest are swallowed up for ever.

The Kingdom of Osiris lies in the west, where the sun sets. Bata will travel there by boat, just as his body went by boat across the Nile on its way to his tomb. The snake goddess Meresger will go with him to protect him from serpents in the other world.

2

The journey to the judgement hall, called the Hall of the Two Truths, is full of danger. Bata will have to pass through many gateways, each guarded by animal-headed gods armed with knives or with the feather that represents truth. To pass the gates he must recite the magic words written in his Book of the Dead.

Men fear death, yet every man can die knowing that he has a chance of a second life. When Bata died, his soul left his body in the shape of a bird. In daytime it can fly back to the land of the living to revisit the places Bata knew when he was alive.

A Plan of the Other World

Most wealthy Egyptians have books of magic called Books of the Dead placed in their tombs, to help them in the after-life. In them are drawings that show what people think the other world looks like. They are plans of the Fields of Yaru—the Egyptian heaven.

The plans show a peaceful land of fields and marshes watered by canals. Virtuous dead people live here among the gods of the spirit world. But they are also expected to work in the fields. This is less pleasant. To avoid having to do it, most rich Egyptians put small statues called *ushabtis* in their tombs. They believe that the *ushabtis* will do the hard work of farming the land for them.

3

In the Hall of the Two Truths, Bata must deny that he did any wrong in his life, before Osiris himself and 42 other judges. The

jackal-headed god Anubis will test his claim by balancing his heart on a scales against the feather of truth. A hideous beast

called the Devourer—part lion, part crocodile, part hippopotamus—waits to swallow him up if he has lied.

4

Ibis-headed Thoth, the scribe of the gods, will note down the result of the trials on his palette. If Bata lied, he would die for ever. But because he was

a good man, he will be taken by the falcon-headed god Horus to the throne of Osiris, to worship him. Then at last his new life in the Fields of Yaru will begin.

The Story of the Pharaohs

The story of the Pharaohs begins 5,000 years ago, in about 3,100 B.C. At that time a warrior king called Menes, from Upper Egypt, conquered the Delta lands of Lower Egypt. He built a new capital city at Memphis, and ruled over the two lands as the first of the Pharaohs.

It was at Saqqara, near Memphis, that the first of the great pyramids was built, 400 years after Menes's death, as a tomb for the Pharaoh Djoser. Before, Pharaohs had been buried in flat-topped brick tombs called mastabas. Djoser's tomb looked like six stone mastabas piled on top of each other. It is known as the Step Pyramid.

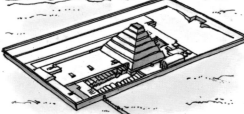

All the great pyramids were built in the next 400 years. The two built at Giza for Cheops and his successor, Chephren, were the biggest of all. They are still the most famous monuments of the Pharaohs, and they were built less than 500 years after Menes joined the two halves of Egypt into one land.

The age when the pyramids were built is known as the Old Kingdom. It was a time of peace and security. Egypt had no powerful foreign rivals to threaten her. The Pharaoh reigned supreme, and the country grew rich. The peasants farmed the land, the priests worshipped the gods. The rich nobles contented themselves with serving the Pharaoh, with looking after their estates and with hunting.

It was the nobles who finally brought the Old Kingdom to an end. They grew so powerful that they no longer respected the Pharaohs at all. The country was split in two and ruled by rival kings, one in the south and one in the north.

This time of troubles lasted for more than 150 years. It came to an end when a new family from Thebes managed to re-unite the land. Peace was restored, and the power of the nobles was checked. This new period of calm is called the Middle Kingdom.

The Middle Kingdom was the second great age of Egypt. It was a time of big engineering exploits, like the draining of the marshy Faiyum. Many of the finest hieroglyphic writings were composed then. Trading ships sailed the Red Sea and the Mediterranean. In the eastern Delta and in Nubia, chains of great fortresses were built to guard Egypt's borders and to protect her troops.

After two and a half centuries of peace, the country was again torn by civil war. The northern and southern halves split, and foreigners, invading from the east, conquered Lower Egypt. The Egyptians called them the Hyksos. They brought with them new weapons, including horses and chariots.

The Hyksos never conquered Thebes. After a century, the rulers of Upper Egypt managed to drive them out of the country by using their own weapons against them. Thebes became the capital of a re-united Egypt. The Theban Pharaohs won back the country's earlier frontiers. Inside Egypt order was restored.

During the first century of the New Kingdom, Egypt had something it had never had before: an effective woman ruler. Queens had reigned before, but only briefly and with little real power. Hatshepsut, however, as regent for her stepson Tuthmose III, took all the power of the Pharaoh for herself. She ruled the country well for 20 years, and built as a monument to herself one of the most wonderful buildings of all Egypt, the temple built into the cliff face at Deir el Bahari.

When Tuthmose III finally took power, the first thing he did was to try to wipe out the memory of the woman who had usurped his powers. He then set out to attack Egypt's enemies abroad. In 15 or more campaigns he built an empire that stretched from Syria to the Sudan. For the first time in her history, Egypt became a great warrior nation.

The empire he built lasted until the end of the long reign of his great-grandson, Amenophis III. It began to crumble under Amenophis's successor, who took the name Akhenaten. Akhenaten was the most revolutionary Pharaoh Egypt ever had. He moved the capital of the land from Thebes to a new city built in the desert, called Akhetaten. Above all, he tried to overthrow the old gods of Egypt, and to replace them with one god, Aten, the Sun's disk.

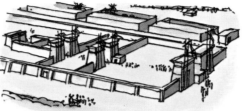

All his efforts were in vain. The religious revolution was stopped during the reign of the boy king Tutankhamen. Amon and all the other gods were worshipped again. Tutankhamen died at the age of 20, but other Pharaohs carried on the work. His successors did their best to wipe Akhenaten's name from people's memories.

In the interval since Amenophis III's reign, Egypt's enemies abroad had grown stronger. It took all the efforts of the last rulers of the New Kingdom to keep them in check. New powers challenged the Pharaoh's armies. They were the Hittites, from what is now Turkey, with whom Rameses II signed a treaty after a long war; and the Sea Peoples of the Mediterranean, defeated in a great naval battle by Rameses III, Egypt's last great warrior king.

After the death of Rameses III, Egypt's great days were over. The country grew gradually weaker as waves of invaders attacked it. The Nubians, subjects of the Egyptians for more than a thousand years, were the first to come. Then it was the turn of the Assyrians, who sacked Thebes in 661 B.C. From time to time strong rulers managed to halt the decay, but never for long. Egypt's next conquerors were the Persians. They were so hated that when Greece's Alexander the Great invaded Egypt to defeat them, he was welcomed as a hero.

After Alexander died, one of his generals, called Ptolemy, took power. He and his heirs ruled Egypt for the next 300 years. The last of the Ptolemys, and the last of the Pharaohs, was the famous Cleopatra. When she killed herself rather than submit to the Roman Octavian, the land became a province of the Roman Empire.

The way of life of ancient Egypt gradually disappeared. Even the great temples fell into decay. Yet its heritage did not die. It had given much to the world, from building and farming to writing and science. Other peoples were able to build on the foundations it left.

29

How We Know About Ancient Egypt

After Egypt became a part of the Roman Empire in 30 B.C., its old way of life came to an end. The people began to worship new gods, and the secrets of hieroglyphic writing were forgotten. Over the centuries, the old temples and palaces became ruins and were covered with sand and rubble.

In the 18th century, travellers from Europe began to take an interest in the past. They went to Egypt to explore the ruined buildings. People began to study hieroglyphics and learned once more how to read them.

Then archaeologists began to dig up the temples and tombs. They learned what Egyptian buildings used to look like, and found wall paintings, scrolls, and objects used in daily life.

People have used all these discoveries like pieces of a jigsaw puzzle, to build up a picture of how the ancient Egyptians lived. The picture is still not complete, but each new find that is made helps to fill the gaps in our knowledge.

This is what the temple of Abu Simbel looked like 150 years ago. The four great statues of Rameses II, for whom it was built, were half covered by earth and sand. Many other famous Egyptian monuments were completely hidden until archaeologists uncovered them.

The first explorers were only interested in spectacular finds, like this huge sculpture of Pharaoh Rameses II. It was dragged to the Nile, then taken to Europe. Early archaeologists did much damage to the buildings that they ransacked in search of treasure. Some even broke open sealed tombs with battering-rams.

How the Hieroglyphic Code was Cracked

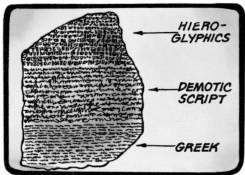

The vital clue to the meaning of the lost language was a stone dug up near Rosetta, in the Delta, in 1799. A message was written on it in Greek and in two kinds of Egyptian writing—including hieroglyphic.

A French scholar called Jean-François Champollion compared the hieroglyphs with the Greek text, which he understood. He worked for 14 years before he made out the meaning of a single word.

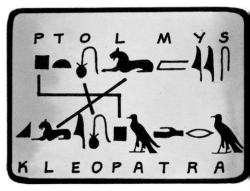

The first word he recognized was 'Ptolemy'—the name of the Greek Pharaohs. By comparing it with the spelling of 'Cleopatra' he worked out the symbols for the letters 'p', 'l' and 'o'.

30

Archaeological Triumph—Tutankhamen's Tomb

The finding of the tomb of the boy Pharaoh Tutankhamen, with most of its treasures inside, was the greatest archaeological discovery of all. It was also a triumph for a new kind of archaeology, very different from the slapdash methods of the early treasure-hunters.

It was found by a patient and determined Englishman called Howard Carter. From what he knew about royal tombs, he was sure that there must still be some undiscovered ones in the Valley of the Kings. With the help of money given by Lord Carnarvon, a wealthy nobleman, he began his search for them.

He worked for five years without finding anything Lord Carnarvon was ready to give up. Carter persuaded him to give the money for one last season's digging. This time, after only four days' work, Carter's men came across steps leading down into the ground.

It did not take very long to dig up the entry to the tomb. Three weeks after the first step was found, Carter made the first opening in the wall blocking up the burial rooms. Holding a candle through it, he peered into the darkness. "Can you see anything?" Lord Carnarvon asked. "Yes," he replied. "Wonderful things."

In fact there were more than 2,000 separate things in the tomb's four rooms, many of them made of gold, like the king's death mask.

On November 4, 1922, Carter first saw the entrance to Tutankhamen's tomb. His workmen uncovered a step while digging under some buried huts. Carter guessed at once that they had found what he had been looking for.

These were the first treasures that Carter saw when he opened the tomb. He later described seeing "strange animals, statues and gold—everywhere the glint of gold." In the centre was a gilded couch shaped like a cow.

This death mask of Tutankhamen was found on his body.

Index

Abu Simbel 30
After-life 25, 26–27
Archaeology 30–31

Beds 9
Bedouin 4, 18
Boats 6, 18–19, 26
Book of the Dead 26–27
Building methods 16, 21
Burial 16, 24–25
Byblos 3, 4, 19

Champollion, J.-F. 30
Canals 6
Canopic chests 24
Carnarvon, Lord 31
Carter, Howard 31
Catch-basins 6–7
Chariots 9, 22–23, 28
Cities 4–5
   Memphis 4–5, 28
   Thebes 4–5, 18, 20, 28–29
Cleopatra 29–30
Crowns 20–21

Dancers 11, 24
Deir el Bahari 5, 29

Faiyum 4–5, 28
Farming 7
Feasts 10–11
Fields of Yaru 27
Fishermen 6
Food 6, 9, 10

Games 9, 21
Gods 13, 26–27
Grain silos 9, 13

Hittites 29
Horses 22, 28
House of Life 13
Houses 8, 19
Hunting 9, 21
   birds 7
   hippos 7
   lions 21
Hyksos 28
Hypostyle hall 12

Kush 5, 20

Land of Punt 5, 18–19

Make-up 10–11
Mastabas 28
Mourners 24
Mud bricks 8
Mummies 25, 26

Nile 4–5, 6–7, 18–19
Nubians 5, 21, 23, 29

Obelisks 12
Ostraca 14

Papyrus 14
Persians 29
Pharaohs 3, 18, 20–21, 22, 28–29
Potters 19
Priests 3, 12–13, 25
Ptolemy 29, 30
Pylons 12
Pyramids 16–17, 28
   Great Pyramid 4, 16–17, 28
   Pyramid of Chephren 17, 28
   Step Pyramid 4, 28

Rameses II 29, 30
Romans 29, 30
Rosetta Stone 30

Sacred lakes 12
Schools 13, 14
Scribes 3, 14, 19, 22
Sea Peoples 29
Servants 3, 8
Shopping 18
Singers 11
Slaves 3, 22
Soldiers 3, 22–23
Sphinx 4, 17
Syria 20

Temples 12–13, 20
Toilets 9
Tombs 17, 24, 21, 31
Trade 4–5, 18–19, 28
Tutankhamen 29, 31

Ushabtis 27

Valley of the Kings 5, 31
Vizier 3, 20
Votive tablets 12

Warfare 22–23
Water clocks 13
Weapons 22–23
Wine 11
Wood 6, 19
Writing 14–15
   Demotic script 30
   Hieratic script 15
   Hieroglyphics 15, 30

Further Reading

If you have enjoyed finding out about the ancient Egyptians, here are some other books you might like to read.

Everyday Life in Ancient Egypt by Jon Manchip White (Batsford)

Pyramid by David Macaulay (Collins)

The Secrets of Tutankhamen by Leonard Cottrell (Evans)

Boy Pharaoh, Tutankhamen by Noel Streatfield (Michael Joseph)

Acknowledgements

This book was prepared in consultation with; W.V. Davies, Assistant Keeper of Egyptian Antiquities for the British Museum; and Dr Anne Millard, author of several books and articles on ancient Egypt, including *The Egyptians* (Macdonald), for children.

First published in 1977 by Usborne Publishing Ltd, Usborne House, 83-85 Saffron Hill, London EC1N 8RT England.

Copyright © 1990, 1977 Usborne Publishing Ltd. Printed in Belgium